DESCRIBING THE PAST

THE ARAB LIST

DESCRIBING THE PAST

Ghassan Zaqtan

TRANSLATED BY SAMUEL WILDER

LONDON   NEW YORK   CALCUTTA

SERIES EDITOR
Hosam Aboul-Ela

Seagull Books, 2016

Originally published in Arabic in 1995

© Ghassan Zaqtan, 1995

English translation © Samuel Wilder, 2016
Foreword © Fady Joudah, 2016

ISBN 978 0 8574 2 349 8

British Library Cataloguing-in-Publication Data
A catalogue record for this book is available from the British Library

Typeset in Bembo Standard by Seagull Books, Calcutta, India
Printed and bound by Hyam Enterprises, Calcutta, India

CONTENTS

By the time Ghassan Zaqtan turned seven years old,
he had become a refugee twice. First, he was born a
refugee in Beit Jala in 1954, six years after the Nakba,
the catastrophe that befell the Palestinian people in
1948 when Israel arose as a state. His family had fled
to Beit Jala from the town of Zakariyya which Israeli
forces had depopulated and demolished that year.
Beit Jala in the West Bank was a small Christian
Palestinian town; and like so many other towns
around it, it had to adjust to abrupt population
growth as it absorb waves of the displaced. Zaqtan's
father worked as a schoolmaster in the nearby
Dheisheh refugee camp. His insistence on founding
a school for girls disturbed some of the local leaders
and led to the family's second dislocation in 1961.
They moved to Karameh refugee camp across from
Jericho, east of the River Jordan. It's in that valley—
its marshes and reeds and flash currents—that
Describing the Past takes place.

Six years passed. And by 1967, another Israeli dispossession resulted in the occupation of the West Bank. Karameh grew larger to accommodate more Palestinian refugees. The camp became a centre of resistance. In 1968, the Battle of Karameh occurred. Israel invaded Jordan and razed the entire camp. The Zaqtan family home was not spared. The setting of Ghassan's childhood became a ghost.

Zaqtan's novella, however, is not that immediately concerned with history. If history is alive and well in the narrative, it mostly serves as spandrel and not arc. What remains, or what emerges as most present is childhood, a childhood whose domain is between the living and the dead. It's a coming-of-age story that ends as soon as it begins in desire. Two teenage boys and a young woman interweave their existence in a refugee camp that holds within it a people's humanity.

Describing the Past is more than an elegy for the death of a childhood friend. And more than lament for the captive sexuality of a young woman and the kindness of an old, pious man. Zaqtan transports memory as dream narrative or, more precisely, as a state of being with altered consciousness. As if in a seance, voices appear and speak from a truncated time, resected and preserved in a jar. The tension is between reflection and a recollection free of it—

reportage that roams in the enduring world of the dead.

Among the many references that Zaqtan's novella conjures, Juan Rulfo's *Pedro Páramo* (1955) comes to mind. The amalgam of details, multiple vistas of single events and their ellipses in *Describing the Past* form a pendulum between reality and phenomenon, a death foretold but unfinished. Physical and metaphysical nostalgia, erotic or otherwise, is a time machine. In a Palestinian context, the travel is to and from a past that won't return, and a present that struggles not to become a persistent past.

Among Palestinian prose, *Describing the Past*, first published in 1994, pays homage to *All That's Left to You*, the classic Ghassan Kanafani wrote in 1966. Both works transform the temporary into the interminable, a fleeing or fleeting eternity. But Zaqtan's novella marks an aesthetic leap. Not much of Palestinian prose has captured the experience of life in a refugee camp with the singular artistic vision of *Describing the Past*.

The proliferative mini-narratives in the novella are memorable: the seventh man, the ablution and breakfast rituals and ceremonies, the basil and mint plants, the unexpected visitation with the coachman's daughter, the ring and the pomegranate, Saint

George and Husseini. All are still lifes that compel rereading. Every exit is a possible point of re-entry.

First and foremost, Zaqtan is a remarkable poet. So much in his poetry recurs and accrues as it returns. Throughout his poems we always encounter houses, pictures of houses, pictures inside them, rooms and hallways, dead boys and girls, ecstasy that has washed itself in the river. With *Describing the Past*, he joins the select company of poets who have augmented their *oeuvre*s with defining prose works. Zaqtan's imperative desire to dissolve life or memory into fiction is an exquisite achievement. He ingests his world to obtain from it the immunity he needs to go on living.

DESCRIBING THE PAST

NOON TEA

I said

It was not easy at all. I had to return. There were so many things left to be done that could no longer be delayed, places where one had to sit, surfaces and peaks of mountains to stare into with strength, narrow and wide roads to walk over, hands to be clasped, many words to be said. There were greetings to be exchanged and a hand with five kind fingers to be laid on your knee so you believe the speech in the air, and birds to be sent across to the others—doves, nightingales, falcons, house sparrows.

To say things like 'good morning,' 'good evening,' and 'peace to you.'

But before everything, to see her.

This was reason enough, so I returned. I went straight towards her, driven by her scent, seized by the fact that she was there. In what came to pass, I went where she was not, beyond her, before her, after her, to the place where her voice could not reach my body, or her scent touch my fingers. As I went, her rough short fingers flashed at my wrist. The seizing mark of the cheap ring on her finger that night remained, burning and flashing. From that moment, my hand remained in loss and my body in absence. I had to free my hand and my body from all that.

I told you already, this started some time ago. She is my loss and she knows this. She is my absence and knows this too.

I told him that before he drowned. Have I told you he drowned? Well yes, he drowned.

Before we weep for him together, she and I. Before I weep for him there, alone. Before I weep for her and him as she sleeps. Before you weep for both of us, for him and me.

I said to him 'She is sleeping in the courtyard almost naked. I saw her with my eyes.'

After he beseeched me in God's name, I told him the whole story. He was silent and swimming in the words, not listening. As I told the story, he saw; and I knew he saw.

The doorway was open as we came back from morning prayers in the mosque—my father, the Hadj and I. My father and the Hadj stopped, and through the open door we saw her sleeping, stretched on the bench, with the light covers pushed away from her legs. Her knee was bent. You couldn't see everything in the half-light, but you could extend and add to it. You could go beyond the revealed if you wanted to, or better if you knew what to imagine.

The next night, we waited for her to fall asleep. We waited for three hours after the evening prayers, then another hour after the lamp went out. We climbed the wall and stared at her body, dark, in sleep, at the far end of the room. We heard the Hadj's snoring rise from a corner of the room we couldn't see. Then I felt her fingers on my wrist. Not *her* fingers at first but rough strong fingers that later became hers. My friend jumped like a cat off the short wall. I trembled. And she kept squeezing. She breathed hard as the metal ring furrowed in my skin, not a ring at first but some sharp instrument that later became a ring.

'What have you come to steal from the Hadj's house, Christian?'

Have I told you that my nickname is Christian?

'Nothing,' I said.

'Then what have you come here to do?'

'Nothing. Nothing.'

We were silent. Her fingers stayed clasped at my wrist, the ring planted itself deeply and slowly in my flesh. I stared at the sleeping body, everything evaporated. The Hadj appeared at the far end of the room, meek and peaceful in sleep, very far away. I said, 'We came to look at you.'

'Am I something to look at, Christian?'

'By God, we came to look at you as you sleep.'

The ring split my flesh and I was in pain.

Her grip loosed for a moment and I escaped through the open door.

A dog in the street barked and ran for the fields, also afraid. We ran on opposite sides of the street, together, until he rushed into a thicket of reeds and his barking grew distant.

I told him everything. I knew he would return there on his own, to the corner of the courtyard, the next day, or the day after that, or some other time. That was what I wanted. I wanted to see him there. But the line ran out between my fingers and I had no power or desire to control it. As I told you, he saw. I saw him alone with her there, or there with *her*. For me it was not easy. For him it was different.

I saw her. All of her. It was painful. Did I tell you that already?

I am compelled to speak now. You know the necessity of it here. Things evaporate and die if they don't find someone to remember them.

I went to borrow a handful of tea. My mother sent me. She said, 'Go borrow a cup of tea from the Hadj's house.'

She gave me a paper funnel to carry the tea. My mother could not live one day without tea.

'Tell them that we'll replace it tomorrow, on Saturday.'

The door was open when I entered, the place was silent. I fear silent houses; our houses are not like that. The silence bewilders me. I said to myself, 'No one is here. She and the Hadj have gone out.'

I was afraid to return without the tea, since my mother would no doubt send me somewhere further away for it, because the tea was so necessary.

I stood perplexed and stared at the doorway to the room where a fabric hung, damp and black and fraying at the edges, doubling for a door. It was hot, as you know, since the sun starts intensely and early in the morning for us. I felt my naked feet burn on cement like molten steel.

I took a couple of steps forward to look through the worn fabric. She was there inside, alone and naked, with a piece of broken mirror in her hand. Her hair was wet, an implausible black, freshly brushed, there was a comb of white bone on the floor. At first she was standing. Then she sat on the floor and leant the mirror against the wall in front of her. Then she stood without the piece of mirror and turned towards me. I froze in my place. I saw her breasts fully and started to cry in silence.

She didn't see me. My feet burnt on the cement. She turned again, picked up the mirror and went to the niche in the wall where we place our lamps. She leant the mirror against the niche's edge and stood on the ends of her toes. She was short and full and brown. She turned around, but didn't see me. She approached the fabric, then turned again, just under my eyes. I heard the sound of her breathing and I trembled.

She was again right in front of my eyes and still didn't see me. She had come back holding the Hadj's bed sheet—no doubt it was his. She folded the fading, broad stripes three times, and stepped onto it to face the mirror.

I was fixed behind the fabric as my eyes welled. Her naked back faced me, her body trembling, sinuous and pulsing with strength. She thrust her lips into the niche, towards the mirror. Her breathing became long and deep. She was in pain. She seemed to be crying. Sobbing. It was not her voice. I fled. I didn't wipe away my tears; I had forgotten them completely. I ran.

She stayed after me, trailing me, behind the doorway and the unfurling fabric, the mirror and the Hadj. She stood on the striped bed sheet, sobbing, alone and naked, trying to come out of the mirror to meet her own lips in a kiss.

I ran and stumbled in the alley and cried.

I was not able. It was not easy. I saw her, all of her, like I told you. I saw her full and alone and harsh in this terrifying way.

THE VOICE'S DESIRE

He said

At first I didn't believe. His concerns were always somewhere else. He was far away and exhausted.

Then he began to talk as we made our way towards the bank of the Sharia river. The sun was hot and dry. It was noon and we had nearly arrived. The vacant hills burst into short tamarisks as we passed through highlands, then flocks of black birds erupted at the river. The hills fell. The tamarisks extended and black birds screamed in greater gatherings. I had taken off my shirt and the scent of wet mud and ground shadows grew dark and more intense as it became hard to walk through the thickening air. The sound of the fast river running through cut the place off completely from everything else around. I took off my pants and was about to rush into the water gleaming in the tunnel through tamarisks when he started to tell the story.

At first I didn't believe it, it was not his voice. There was a strand of fantasy that glimmered in his words, some current of rash hunger and desire, of fear and fraud. Little by little, like dust growing slowly and insistently into heaps, she started to gather there in the voice towards a point of completion. She became clear, and close. I saw her in his voice reclining nude and whole. Her knee flashed at a distance. At the centre of her figure, a dark spot of light amassed, turning and breathing. I was there. I saw her in his voice with a clarity that did not exist for him; she was clearer and more complete in his voice than anything he had looked at or beheld. He told and I saw. He described, stopping only to catch his breath before going on into descriptions, travelling to all regions of her and sending back messages to me, granting to her some new miracle at every instance. The river jumped in front of us like a kid racing from the herd. I was completely naked.

I never paid attention to her before that. She was greater than us, distant and secluded, always wrapped in odd clothing that must have once belonged to her now-dead mother, old and worn-out clothes that somehow became new when she put them on. Withdrawn and utterly apart, in retreat; she was not concerned. In her brown skin she was protected and hidden. No desire to be important, no effort to be so. It was impossible. Really, at that time I could not recall anything—of her eyes, eyelashes, lips or nose. I knew her walk. I knew her form. A strong memory of her entering the open doorway of her house, how she passed through the empty space before the door, never turning, then vanished completely as if the first touch of the house air had dissolved her. Her house was shockingly silent and abandoned. Inside it, she and the Hadj never moved at the same time. Only one of them could move while the other remained still, as if in silence they had divided between themselves the power to move, to bend and walk through that air.

Or as if invisible creatures had put everything into order for them, divided all the tasks, the food, the washing, the sleep, the speech.

Once or twice I entered for reasons I don't recall, to retrieve a ball or something like that. We forget such things, but I will try to remember later on.

The room was orderly, neat and exceptionally clean. Nothing lived inside. The invisible creatures had accomplished their tasks and returned to absence.

Her walk, only her walk, is how I must begin when I remember her. Then her short, tense, locked form vanishing once it passed through the open doorway.

As he spoke, he saw her and touched her with his voice. The voice is the scandalized and bewildered realization of a thing. The tone describes and grants and draws. I saw her wholly in his voice, without the dead woman's aged clothing or the hardness of her walk, without the Hadj. She stood before everyone, veiling and banishing them with her silence. As the river flashed through the narrow tunnel of tamarisks, she flashed in his voice. I saw her in the parts and bends of the sound, opening, quietly undressing in front of me with confidence. She was alone, wronged, cruel. In his voice, I loved her and knew she was greater than us.

On the river's edge she became clear and captivating.

And she stays there, suspended in the air, between his voice and the surface of the river, described as a woman like her must be described.

She said

I awoke from sleep. Something woke me. A sound or a call, a strange movement, five fingers on a lithe hand.

Someone woke me.

The muezzin was at the end of the call. Then everything fell silent.

The house was empty without reason.

I looked at the bed and he was still there. I crawled on my knees to him.

The void multiplied. He was dead.

I put the cover back on his face and went barefoot to the doorstep. The imam had begun the prayer. 'Amen' opened like a tremendous canopy over the houses.

The alley was dark and empty. The scent of guava, orange and mint fanned from the river and weighed down the air. I opened the front of my dress to breathe, but it wasn't enough, so I tore it down to the waist and left everything open to the thick smell.

I was alone and free and silent, with the Hadj inside, covered up to his forehead.

Water drops gathered and started to run in slow hesitant pulses like affectionate fingers lost in the pleasure of touch.

I shut my eyes and slept in the doorway as the void grew behind me in the room, over the court-yard and above the Hadj. All I could think was how drops of dew gathered on my breasts and ran down between them, loaded with the scent of fruit.

The Hadj was dead inside.

The Hadj who had never been but dead, his long string of blue prayer beads was dead now too, all ninety-nine sisters, the whole family, every single member dead—the Hadj, his fingers, the prayer beads.

I will never take account again, wherever I am, of the years between us, as the beads move in his hand, wherever he is, will never again count the years of giant silence.

From where I was, I could see the high palms of Abu Mashrif, the female ones, their fronds held in clusters.

With the coming of light, I passed through the threshold, went into the room, lifted the cover from his face and kissed his forehead, so ancient, from a distant time I didn't remember.

During the last years, I no longer looked at his face. I had learnt it by heart completely, recalled it like reading the Al-Fatiha from memory. In the rhythm at its core, the sura pours its dark, guarded and intuitive power. The seven verses pour to the final purity and protection of 'Amen'.

In death, he was meek and content. Some strands of embarrassment glimmered in his face, an apology perhaps for the small trouble he would cause after his death, the unintended but needed effort for me to realize that he, too, no longer exists.

He was there as he had lived. He had lived on the soft pads of his feet, as he passed now along the edge of death—not through it but alongside its edge, as he had passed beside life, simple and small and content. A narrow passage seemed to open in the air to let him through.

He looked perplexed, just as he had on the evening when he said to my mother, 'You are alone, Hadja, and the girl will go astray when you are gone. Marry her to me in the ways of God and His Prophet, let her eat and drink and be protected, and when I die, she will have the means to live and will have understood life.'

Now he is dead as promised—dead, silent and just.

I shut his eyes and kissed them. I put the cover on his face. I went out after I gathered my torn clothes. The sun was about to rise. The air was still. Another burning day to begin.

I came to the third doorway on the right, your house. I wanted you to be the first to know. I wanted to say to you, 'The Hadj is dead.'

I wanted you to be sad with all your heart.

I said

'Before everything, I had to see her. That's why I returned.'

When I arrived, she was going up a narrow dusty road. Behind her, the river was distant and visible and radiant. Her walk had slowed and become heavier. She seemed shorter. A fine trail of dust flew behind her as if the wind were sculpting her body, blowing on her taut skin and fanning it into a small and tender storm. She carried her child on her chest. They had married after the Hadj's death and she bore a child. On her head she carried a wicker basket. She was exhausted, gone, erased by her burdens—but she didn't know this. She paid no attention to such details and never cared to. The road was narrow and uncovered, full of dust and exhaustingly straight.

I said, 'Hand me the boy.'

'He is asleep.'

Her voice came unhurried, calm and deep. It ran down through her burdens without meaning, mixed with the straw and the vegetables, passed through her breast and the child's body.

I said, 'Don't be afraid, I'll help you.'

I reached out my hand to take the small, curled body. Her chest came close. Her breasts touched my fingers in two places, and I felt her trembling through the shirt that was no doubt his. Now, she wore the clothes of her three dead—his shirt, her mother's handkerchief, the Hadj's shoes.

The boy didn't wake up but adjusted into a new curl, passed his little hand into my shirt to grope for a corner to snuggle. With his hopes dashed, he retuned to contentment and fell asleep. I felt then that I had left her exposed, uncovered. Even without looking I was certain that her chest was bare and alive. I knew everyone stared, and that dust flew from the unseen bodies all around us and gathered on her breasts. Dust flew from astonished and frightened eyes as she came to my side in silence, her chest bare and alive.

On her other side, he was walking in death. Behind him, on the road of dust, a strand of river water poured from his hair and body. He was silent. Behind us the Hadj walked. I slowed down and she and he followed my lead, slowed down so that the Hadj could catch up to us. He was silent too. Three men surrounded her. All four of us kept climbing.

I was going off to die. That's what I was told. She didn't know this, but the two men did. We three dead men surrounded her as we climbed the narrow, straight road of dust. The river was behind us, and she among us was with bare torso as the dust came to gather. Orange and weightless dust piled on her breasts and ribs. Blue dust flew from her shoulders, dissipating in the air. The two of them looked on and I tried to preserve the entire moment, to take it in, this place where they were. The Hadj caught up to us and she let him walk between herself and me, leaving the other man where he was—on her other side. The strand of water that fell behind my friend picked up momentum. I heard the sound of a lone spout pouring in cold space, falling from a time I didn't know, before I was born, sounding a hopeless, constant, slowed-down descent.

She said, 'I will come by tomorrow and arrange your room.'

She knew, without a doubt.

I said, 'Don't trouble yourself.'

In the same voice, coming directly from her torso, she said, 'Leave the door open and go to the coffee shop or the fields if you like.'

Yes then, she knew.

'As you wish,' I said.

Then she pressed her bare torso and the river was naked behind us. She walked faster and we her guards, her three dead, increased the pace. From somewhere the dust converged above and the spout kept pouring. Alone and patient, I said, 'Why did the Hadja not come?'

She did not hear or answer and I did not repeat the question.

He said

I went back on my own. I entered through the door which was always open. First I heard the snoring of the Hadj and then I saw her gather at the far end of the dim room. She started to move towards me. I didn't move from where I stood. I was going nowhere but here, towards her. She asked the darkness, 'Christian?'

She searched for a lone, decisive 'yes', a 'yes' complete with ten fingers and eyes and mouth. In my darkness, I said, 'No.'

She said, 'Go back to the house.'

'What house?' I said.

'Your house.'

I remained standing, fortified in my darkness as she came towards me.

'Are you the Iraqi's son?'

The nickname 'the Iraqi' had been attached to my family for some years now because of my eldest uncle. He talked constantly about his role in helping the Iraqi army towards the end of the 1948 war, north of the West Bank. The basis of my uncle's story was that he served in the region as a guide to an artillery regiment that had altered the course of the war and protected a number of villages in the sector (my uncle called it a 'sector') from massacres, forced migration and complete annihilation, which was the fate of hundreds of towns that year on the coast, in Galilee and Jerusalem. The historical truth of the role played by those five or six regiments was not in question. The inhabitants of those areas had even taken the rare step of erecting a monument to the Iraqi troops killed in the battles that summer. Flowers travelled to the monument from towns and the far, calm reaches of the hills and valleys. Wildflowers, oleander, flowers of tenderness, olive twigs held by farmers across mountain passes of dust and thorn.

Those days were retold by the bread of many houses, in the stories and treasures of many men. But hesitation followed when it came to discussing my uncle's role in all that. Those few weeks that he spent with the artillery regiment were the only thing that gave him any peace in a life that had been mostly without satisfaction.

If he went astray in his story, or if he felt that the listener was not sufficiently convinced, he seasoned the events with words of Iraqi dialect, giving touches of flavour that usually pleased the listener. He called the officers by their first names and paid no attention whatsoever to ordinary soldiers, whom he mercilessly and conspicuously left out. This seemed to glorify his own position, which was very eagerly delineated in the telling. It did not seem to matter to him how this neglect of the ordinary soldiers affected the impression of the structure and hierarchy of the Iraqi army in general, or at least of that particular regiment, which seemed to consist of an innumerable cast of officers and holders of high rank moving against a vague background of faded, indistinct troops. A dazzling light was cast on the few officers who were his focus—we learnt their names, traits, positions and behaviours to a point of complete familiarity. The listener could effortlessly bring to mind the scene of Abu al-Jasim (the Iraqis' nickname for Muhammad) creeping leopard-like over the rocks, penetrating regions of jujube trees and shrubby mountain thorns, up to the closest reach of the enemy, until he could hear their chatter and smell their tea. 'Abu al-Jasim knew Hebrew as well as the Jews, maybe better,' my uncle would say. Then he would fall silent, distracted for a moment, and look into our faces for signs of the impact of what he had said.

There were wide and painful, overlapping gaps in the story. But the intense desire of the listeners to break apart the lost war into tiny heroisms, each holding a private victory, alongside my uncle's piercing faculty for performance and effect, turned those doubtful events with one witness into rooted, living truth. The officers became our loved ones next door.

The climax of the story came when Abu al-Jasim wept into my uncle's hands, 'balling like a woman' because he 'had no orders'.

The story of some Iraqi officers crying is established and well known in the area. This occurred when orders were issued for them to cease fighting and march down to the sea, to leave matters as they stood on the ground. There was no convincing justification given for those orders, especially not in a war like this, which had become a holy war for the officers.

What was very doubtful, however, was that this crying took place between my uncle's hands.

It further weakened the story among sceptics that our family did not belong to this region originally but had come from the hills overlooking the coast in the south. It was difficult to imagine how a man who was born and lived in the south could come to work as a guide to a regiment conducting military operations in the north.

Clearly, he had chosen the one point of victory in that impossible war and decided to become a participant in it—maybe because the defeat was so sudden and heavy, beyond what one could anticipate or handle.

Then the Iraqi vocabulary became more widespread in his stories, like small nails used to fix the days into place. Little by little, the words crept into his daily language. He gave an obviously Iraqi name to one of my cousins, against my father's reservations and to my mother's astonishment.

At the next stage, he was able to convince my father to buy one of the few radio sets in the camp, and the dial never strayed from the Iraqi broadcasting station. We listened to news from the Iraqi provinces about discoveries of oil, electricity and water projects, paving of roads and agricultural projects, building of bridges, the water levels of the Tigris and Euphrates, the temperatures in Baghdad, Basra and Kirkuk.

The music played in our house was Iraqi. Nazim al-Ghazali, Zuhur Hussein and Sadiqa al-Moulaya were well-known personalities in our house, filling it with Iraqi songs. Bizarre lines of thought crept into my uncle's narrations, never really clarified, linking our family's roots to Iraqi tribes that migrated at some unknown time into Palestine. The time of our migration moved up to around the turn of the century, closer and closer to the present day.

These strands of thought multiplied until a new contiguous story arose, with its own pathways and causalities and events. At scattered times, my uncle announced that he wanted to go back. According to him, the sons of some uncle were searching for us frantically, asking for us everywhere. His desire to go to Iraq became more intense. He would strike up conversations with the drivers of big rig trucks headed across the Syrian desert through Iraq, towards Kuwait.

Strange yet profound relationships developed with the drivers, some of whom started to frequent our house. Gifts started to arrive—manna dew, dates, tamarind, tamarind honey, spice blend, cardamom seeds, Basra lemons. Through all this, he never stopped talking of his few weeks guiding the regiment. We discovered suddenly that we had become the house of 'the Iraqi', and we put up no protest at all. The existence of Iraq, so complete and so near, the vast and dark country, gave us peace, and gave us a deep desire to go there one day. My uncle nurtured this dream. He promised us all that we would study there.

My uncle—he never married and never went to Iraq, but he gave us that name for ever. She called me by that name that night.

I said, 'Yes.'

She came close and spoke into my eyes. She was not afraid. Her breath touched my face. She said, 'Why don't you go wait for your friend in the alley?'

She had come very close. I grabbed her arms just above the wrists as we were about the same height.

For a moment, she drew back and I felt the strong muscles of her body contract against my fingers. But I kept the pressure. There was nothing else I could do. I could not set her hands free. She knew all this. Suddenly she went slack, not in weakness or surrender but peacefully. The tension in her muscles relaxed, the sound of her breathing rose and she canted her head powerfully.

Then she looked towards the room. The snoring of the Hadj reached us. She wrested her arms free from my fingers, took me by the hand, no, the wrist, and pulled me to the corner of the courtyard. I walked behind her, led by my captured hand. From there we could see the Hadj's meek body in the dim and bobbing light. I collided with the row of basil bushes, and the contact released a penetrating scent. Its flood cordoned the corner off from the rest of the place.

She said, 'Make no sound. No sound at all.'

WITNESSING

She **said**

The Hadj came to the door after evening prayers. He asked permission to come in and then came in. He was with a marriage official and two friends acting as witnesses. I was in the kitchen when they sat on the bench. My mother was there. The official rose and passed through the courtyard, towards the kitchen, with my mother and the two witnesses. My mother stood in the darkness. The marriage official came in.

He was a short man and I could see the witnesses over his shoulders. Deliberate and disinterested, he asked me if I accepted the Hadj as my husband. He looked remarkably similar to the old man. I couldn't answer, but I stared over his shoulders at the witnesses who also looked similar to the Hadj. I was in the light. My mother was in the dark.

The official said, 'With God's blessing.'

He turned to follow the witnesses, and my mother, out of the darkness, joined him. From where I was, I saw the Hadj seated on the bench, still hunched over and running the prayer beads through his fingers. He had been on that bench, waiting for them since a distant time, alone and frail and kind to the furthest degree.

They climbed the two steps to the bench where the Hadj was seated and gathered: the marriage official, then the witnesses, then my mother.

The voice of the official said, 'With blessings, Hadj.'

Then I heard the voice of the witnesses; then my mother's voice: 'With blessings, Hadj.' 'With blessings, Hadj.'

All this took but a few minutes. The agreement had occurred a week before between my mother and the Hadj, and I knew this.

The two of them were now discussing something else, and the Hadj was speaking.

WE CAME TO WATCH YOU SLEEP

I said

On the way from the house to the coffee shop, the view of the alleys was different. The eyes of the people were different. Something new and bottomless was embedded in sound and vision. The sounds were altered. Waves moved through the air with caution and control, as if afraid to reach my body and wound it, to set death flowing down my clothes and spilling onto the street. I felt the lightest sense of touch, a chaste pilfering that followed looks of sadness. 'Good morning' was closer to 'go in peace.' I felt the enticing sting of the curious gaze that approached in stealth, guarded by the onlookers' dark desire, a desire not free of malice.

Three women stopped. One of them was almost crying, and one of them greeted me in a raised and hurt voice. A woman I didn't know looked at me, and her gaze stood long and precise in my eye. Then suddenly, as if seeing a bucket rise after a year from a well's darkness, she exclaimed, 'Good morning, sir.'

The third woman smiled with a sturdy weariness as if about to die.

I felt I had signed out of the agreement entirely, without my will or theirs. I was no longer there. I was not there. Not to the woman who said 'Good morning' to a dead man, and not to her two friends— the one who almost cried and the one about to die. They reeled their vision over a dead man who was free of contracts and beyond blame. It was then that my existence became lighter, my movements bolder. My eyes went wherever I wanted them to go.

The children piled around and on top of one another in the roundabout and didn't return my greeting, but kept staring at my walk. They didn't hear the 'good morning' and didn't believe the hand that I raised to angle it to them, to guide it to them or them to it.

The man who owned the barber shop, the barber, seemed drawn away in fear in the depths of his shop. His eyes flashed and were apprehensive. He seemed to be waiting eagerly, with desire or expectation, for me to fall and dwindle into nothing, or fly away.

To him too I said, 'Good morning.'

He murmured, busied himself, set his hands in motion as if afraid for my dead voice to reach him.

The bicycle renter stood between two boys, admonishing them. He was chiding some wrong thing one of them had done—probably the shorter one whose head was lowered. Despite his subjection, I saw his eyes beam and widen, full of colour, stealing glances towards me.

I said to him and to the two of them, 'Good morning.'

I waved my hand at a phantom behind the coachman's window, and the phantom behind the window waved back.

The memory that she is there now. The meaning of it. The power of her presence there, the obscure energy of the notion that she is there now, moving through my room as she is and as she was, in his fading shirt, in her mother's rags and the Hadj's shoes. Her short unwavering steps spread her vitality through the air as she bends over the table, flips through books on the shelf and regrets that she cannot read.

She is there alone—with all those private possessions, with the things I have thought about constantly and withdrawn from every moment, with all the intentions and all the desires swimming around her in the air.

In the corner, I left a small striped bed sheet and a piece of a mirror that she had broken last evening. I tossed a black fabric by the doorstep, its hem made loose by my fingers. In the niche was a comb made of white bone. It was nearly everything she would need, or everything she should need. I did away with everything else, everything that could distract me.

I sat in the wicker seat in the coffee shop, serene and silent. With every bit of concentration I could summon, my thoughts channelled to the noon of many years ago. I saw her atop the backless wicker chairs. She turned around but did not see me. She cried, and then it turned into a high wail heard from a new position. I was fixed behind the weightless, unfurling fabric like a statue with seeing eyes. I stared at her naked shining back, her hair black beyond belief and the teeth of the white comb. She was occupied, far off in the mirror. The whole time, I watched her strong short fingers, full, pliant, experienced.

That, and only that, was everything I needed, what I think about, what I cannot stop thinking about. It is what I turn over and over in this hemmed-in and blockaded life, what makes the whole thing bearable and believable.

I returned early, before the kids had come back from school. I pushed open the door and walked into the courtyard. Her fingers were everywhere within, on the clothes hung delicately on the wall, on the books, on the shelf, and on the reading glasses that I had not used for so long.

Her strong, supple, painstaking fingers were etched with clarity into my wrist from that night. I looked down to be sure. Five fingers shone at my wrist, a cheap silver-plated ring flickered.

I heard my voice hoarse and afraid, alone there in the darkness. 'I swear to God, we came to watch you while you sleep.'

He said

I stood next to the short Christ's thorn. She was at the far end of the courtyard, on the ground damp from the jar of water that sat there. She grabbed the jar, shook it empty over the basin of mint, sprinkled the basil leaves whose tremor let a penetrating, singular scent rush out.

I was about to tell her that I was on my way to the river to meet Omar who was waiting for me by the Abu Mashrif palms. She never liked it when I went to the river with Omar. Omar became my new friend after the other one went away—I don't know where to. Omar and I were on the same team at the club, and he was by far the better sport. In weight-lifting, he was a natural champion. His gifted body, his silence. He was shy of his own voice. Few people ever heard enough of Omar's voice, and I was one of them.

He would begin to speak suddenly, usually when we were alone and headed down towards the valley and the great rock. There was speech in the air in front of us and between us. I gathered it and rearranged it as we walked.

I loved Omar's voice. Voices interest me a great deal. Voice giving the sign of the thing, the other being, close and connected. Omar's voice was kind and shy, but with a dark rashness somewhere in its layers.

Later on, he killed his sister.

As I was saying, I used to watch her shake the jar in the damp corner of the courtyard. At the time, she was full and tense inside her shining brown skin. She breathed with a high sound that reached me, one whole sound, enveloped in the scent of basil. I thought also of her fingers, so short and strong and rough. I saw her standing in the middle of the court-yard. She lifted up the corner of her dress and tucked it in her underwear, then shook the jar again. She was engrossed in that act, put her whole body into it. She did not see me standing there by the Christ's thorn, with my open eyes and astonished face.

Her body moved in a repetitive sequence like a short, uncoiling viper. This gave even more shine to the details of her body beneath the damp dress that stuck to her in several places. She was strong and I loved her strength. She was capable of effort, of becoming absorbed in an act. She had a nimbleness that diffused a certain pleasure through her torso and eyes. She never ceased to be beautiful and captivating when she was tense at work. This is what gave off the idea—which her body conveyed to me—that there was joy on the road. I stood there. I had not yet told her that I was going to the river to meet Omar. She was thirty, on the short side, with a strong body and wild eyes that did not see me. Her dress was wet.

Somewhere else, in some other time, two strands of water flowed from the vine of her loose and incredible black hair. The two strands flowed, twisting about her ears to her torso, through the deep passage between the rises of her breasts.

She spotted me. She spotted me and laughed, and none of it had any particular meaning. But I was afraid.

I heard the door close behind her. Before that I heard her voice. Then I went to Omar, waiting for me for some time under the palms of Abu Mashrif.

AMEN

She said

We moved into the Hadj's house. We sold our house to one of his friends, then a small pickup came and we loaded up everything we had. The pickup crossed the river by Allenby Bridge and I arrived here with my mother.

The Hadj put the money from the sale of the house into a secure trade with one of his friends, and we began our life. At first, we were in another house by the river where the Hadj had been since the death of his first wife. But then he started to build this house, closer to the people, so that I wouldn't feel so alone by the river.

In the early days, my mother slept in the kitchen, and the Hadj and I slept in the room. We went to bed just after the evening prayers. At the first benedictions before the dawn call to prayer, the two of them would rise, each from their darkness, and go at once towards their green and red plastic water pitchers—green for the Hadj and red for my mother—to begin their day.

'We wake, and possession is God's.'

'Good morning, Hadj.'

'Good morning, Hadja.'

The Hadj would go first. He would hold the green pitcher and go. Then my mother. She would hold the red pitcher and go. The Hadj then headed to the mosque while my mother prayed on the bench. She would turn her small mat in the direction of Mecca, and with audible voice recite the benedictions, open her palms and begin the invocations. Then she would rise, gather the prayer rug and go into the room to arrange the Hadj's bedding, taking care not to wake me.

She would go to the kitchen where I could hear her light the burner and put on the pitcher of tea, getting ready to prepare breakfast. When she heard his footsteps, the drag of his slippers in the alley, she carried the straw tray to the bench. He would clear his throat at the doorway, and she would beckon him in.

'With God's acceptance, Hadj.'

'With God's acceptance, Hadja.'

She would entreat him to start his breakfast, and he beseeched her to join him so that they might breakfast together. Then they would begin to chat. Every morning I waited for this, observed it from the same spot in my room. They would go into every subject, almost every subject—religion, life, the earth, the weather, the country that they had left behind. They began with the description of paradise, then recalled the dead, the murdered, the migration routes that were taken, the three seedlings of sweet basil planted by my mother in the corner of the courtyard.

The Hadj told stories of the Prophet and his wife Aisha, of the Companions, and the heroic deeds of Ali. Mother sat in silence, spellbound, in front of his teeming, various world. I heard it all in my sleep. I saw the holy Ali, I called out to Asma of the Two Sashes, I saw Ja'far the Flyer, Suleiman the Knight, Bilal the Abyssinian and the people of Yasir.

Then the Hadj began to chant the Quran, his voice deep and strange, his pose cross-legged as my mother submitted to a trance not far from him, at the edge of the bench. I swam through the weightless air around them. After 'God's Great Truth,' the Hadj began the invocation in a different voice. My mother waited for the end of the invocation before she muttered from where she sat on the bench, 'Amen.'

Under my covers, I repeated urgently, 'Amen. Amen.'

When I arose after the sun's rays, I felt in the air around me the chants of the Hadj, his simple and acute invocations.

The Hadj always mentioned his first wife with kindness. The words 'the deceased' signified her exclusively among all his dead, and all the dead of the Muslims. He spoke about her to my mother in their long sessions on the bench or at the doorway in the evenings, after she had swept the threshold and sprinkled its dust with water and once she had brought out the old straw mat and spread it before the doorstep. On the mat, she placed a small side-cushion and pillow for the Hadj to recline as she sat in the doorway. I sat next to her, my head silent on her shoulder, and listened to their voices move in their world of magic and belief.

My mother spoke to the Hadj about her first husband, my father, who was killed by the Haganah in 1948. She said they took him out of the English prison with six other young men. They handed the smallest one a shovel and told him to start digging a long trench. When he finished, they shot him into it.

They forced the remaining ones to cover him with earth using their hands. When they had done this, they handed the shovel to the second. This went on until they reached the seventh. When he had dug his own grave, they left him alive to tell the village.

My father was the fifth, the seventh had later said.

In those days, my mother said, there were many sevenths wandering through villages, sitting on wells and roadstones, telling stories like this or different.

Wrapped in fear and grey-haired, they rushed towards the east. The Hadj remembered a woman passing through their village that summer. She insisted that there was a child in her arms, and screamed at the other child behind her, who was holding on to her dress, slowing her down. The Hadj said, 'We stared at her empty arms and torn clothes. We asked mercy of God. Her hair was like snow. Later, we learnt that they had slaughtered her two boys in front of her, and released her to tell the villages.'

There were so many murdered, everywhere, in 1948. Men, women, children, whole villages with names and traits and memories—they ended and died. All of them came to our doorstep, and my father too, all of them breathed in silence.

And at dawn, the dead would bow down with the rest of the house to listen to the chanting and invocations of the Hadj. They repeated along with me, my mother and the three shrubs of basil, 'Amen. Amen.'

DROWNING

He said

I was busy with the small one when she entered. She spoke little, only words of extreme need. She went straight into the kitchen, silent and strong and unworried. I heard the gas burner light, then overlapping sounds in close successions that I arranged in order:

First, she filled the water heater a little over halfway.

Second, she put the heater on the burner and arranged its position.

Third, she moved plates on the wooden shelves.

She came out with a straw tray holding plates of onions, olives, oil, thyme, sliced tomato and cucumber. She put it in front of me and said, 'Have your supper.'

And *he* said

Her voice was gripping and surprising. I couldn't make out her face. A light broke through the locks of her hair and lit her shoulders. Shadows crept away down her neck.

The burner hissed in the kitchen as she passed me and I felt her, weightless, at my side. In her hand was a bundle of clothes and a fabric that she put up on the kitchen door. Her voice could be heard as she was cooling the water on the stove. She attempted the tune of some popular song. Her voice was not as sweet when she sang as you would imagine from her speaking. The sounds continued. Water splashing from kettle to cup, then breaking on the cement floor and the brass tray.

And *he* also said

There was a cold spray from her hair and the scent of soap when she passed by me. Everything must have been put in order in the kitchen by now—the floor clean and shining, the brass tray turned over and leant against the wall. And her scent, a taut body washed with olive soap.

That's when I felt fear and despair, lingering of a terrible loss. A place deep and flooding. I don't know how I got there.

THE COACHMAN'S HOUSE
AND DAUGHTER

I said

I had become completely light. Things kept changing. I was able to break through the familiar and go past it. I was outside the agreement, utterly tolerated, enveloped in some kind of multiplying and sufficient pardon.

I had begun to take pleasure in all this. I knew that some new agreement had been formed between me and them, that some day not far off I would have to die, and that I would have to carry, at the same time, the full burden of all these looks of pity, curiosity and bewilderment, including, no doubt, in the eyes of the barber.

'Good evening,' I said to the bicycle renter. From far off I could see the oil sheen in his hair, then from closer three gold teeth flashed in his mouth. As I approached, the oil scent wafted from his hair and face, from his neck and chest. When I passed him, after 'good evening,' I saw red lines in his eyes, traces of long nights and alcohol.

The two boys ran out from inside the shop and stopped to look at me with astonishment.

I had reached the alley of the coachman's house. His daughter appeared at the window.

For many years I had wanted to go in. Here I used to break my stride and jump off of my toes. Inside the window, I could catch sight of the still-life painting of fruit and of 'God's majesty exalted' in gilded Kufic script near the top of the inside wall. Later on, I only had to stand straight on the balls of my feet to see inside. Finally, when I grew even taller, I could approach the window and quickly glance over the dark furnishings of the room. That was by the end of preparatory school.

The coachman's house was similar to the other surrounding houses. A bedroom, a kitchen, a covered patio, a narrow courtyard. The main window was low and looked out on the alley, with a smooth metal screen to keep away gnats and mosquitoes in the summer months. All our windows had these coverings, the 'sieve' we called it, which also cut off the view.

Since the time we discovered it in our youth, when we climbed and meddled and believed in anything, the coachman's house had remained special and different, drawn with miraculous accuracy, always with the two-wheeled car leaning against its wall next to the doorway. The whole adjacent area had been scratched away by the transport of strange furnishings into the house.

Things passed through the gate after a little manoeuvring to avoid the two-wheeled vehicle. The passing objects gave a constant low ring, gathering from a distant time when we were young, or are young still, a time when everything was believable, or at least everything that was told to us. Everyone helped these objects along, passed everything they could carry, embellished them with awe and ambiguity, with visions and odd narratives whose protagonist was always the only witness. The house returned nothing. It swallowed whatever came to it, took from our hands and added to its possessions and stories and furnishings, and, thus, swelled into a house of sorcery rather than the home of a widowed coachman with only one daughter.

The house was also outside the agreement— tolerated, offering forgiveness, safeguarded in its necessary difference. Its existence in that spot seemed like some kind of intuitive barrier to the flow of the objects that surrounded it: the house of Omar the shoemaker, the bicycle rental shop at the corner and the barber's shop.

'Come in, sir.' The coachman's daughter spoke from behind the sieve. I was going forward, about to pass into this entity. It seemed so intimate and trust-worthy and complete. The young woman rose behind the sieve and went out of the room, then appeared at the doorway to repeat the words, 'Come in, sir.'

As she raised her voice, her eyes passed over me towards the bicycle renter. I went through the door-way, leaving the alley, the two-wheeled car and the patio. I sat down on the only reed bench, behind the sieve. From there, I could see one side of the main street and the beginning of the alley.

The bicycle renter bent over an incredibly gigantic tricycle, with the two boys around him. In their hands and on the ground around them were tools, screwdrivers, wrenches of every size, screws and rags.

The voice of Abdel Halim Hafez rose from the barber shop on the radio.

Inside the house, high up on the wall near the ceiling, was a print of a still life of a tropical fruit. In our house, at nearly the same place, hung a picture of Abd al-Qader al-Husseini posing in gun belt with a white keffiyeh on his head.

On the other wall was a piece of pasteboard on which 'God's majesty exalted' was written in Kufic script. At that corresponding spot in our house, there was a print of a folk drawing of Khidr or Saint George slaying the dragon. Nearby, on a table of sculpted dark olive wood, there was a carved statuette showing the same scene. As she sat and knitted in the shadows, my mother would start to sing,

> *O Khidr you green one*
> *O prophet David*
> *Guard the brown boy*
> *With his jet-black eyes.*

In the corner of the room was a precious, pampered cabinet. It was a dark brown wood that shone as if just rubbed with olive oil. A short and neat throw-fabric with imbricate lace-work edges covered its top. Behind its glass doors was a set of ornamental china, arranged around a gilded frame. In the black-and-white picture, a woman stood leaning on a horse-drawn carriage. She wore a black dress with short sleeves and a long opening at the chest. The woman's hair was pressed into waves in the 1930s style. I pointed to the picture, but before I could ask, she said, 'This is my mother, sir.'

She stood up carefully and took the picture from behind the glass. With the back of her hand she brushed away the dust that did not exist. She stared at the woman, then handed her to me.

The woman came out of the picture. She invaded the house, the room and the features of the girl sitting across from me; she was living, immediate and cherished. The coachman on the other hand I could find nowhere. His traces and movements and voice were not in that place; he was not there. The house was possessed by the pictured, possessed by the woman who stood there leaning with special allure against the horse-drawn coach in her black dress with her hair in waves.

Dust started to come through the window. Fine dust gathered on my hand, on the picture and the horse's neck, on the shoulders of the girl, on the still life of tropical fruit and the curves of the Kufic script. From a distant time, the dust had gathered on the spear of Saint George and Husseini's gun belts, on the dark wood of the table and on my mother's needle and embroidery and hymn.

I sat within the whirl, at its core. Dust grew on me and gathered on the pavement of the town square in the picture, the pavement that had been bright moments ago.

I said, 'You are from Jaffa?'

She said, 'Yes. That's where this picture was taken.'

Before the migration, I realized.

She was confounded and silent. She had put waves in her hair and put on a black dress with short sleeves and a collar that revealed a long stretch of her lean chest.

At the corner, the bicycle renter squatted between the boys. The taller one poured water on his hands from a yellow plastic pitcher while the shorter one carried a towel. A child went off on the incredible tricycle.

Across the way, the barber shook dry a towel at the doorway of his shop and stared towards the window where I sat behind the sieve, the picture of the woman from Jaffa in my hands. Exactly across from me, outside the gilded frame of the picture, stood a perplexed girl who resembled her, a girl who had just come out of the picture. I saw her missing in the picture—an empty space between the woman and the horse. That was where she had been, no doubt, before I arrived, and she would return there as soon as I leave, to stand there with her mother. I saw empty space there too, in the town square, for the bicycle renter, the two boys and the barber shop.

To the bicycle renter I said, 'Good evening.'

He had just finished washing and drying his hands. He sat now on a backless wicker chair, in front of a turned-over tin can, on top of which was a tray of teacups. Behind him, bicycles of different sizes were leant against the wall, and past that I could see the narrow, clustered coffee shop. No doubt the two boys—the tall one with his blue pants blotted with grease and oil, and the short one in his long apron— were busy inside repairing wheels, patching and inflating tyres, oiling chains and fixing them to gears.

Among the many chores these boys did to satisfy their boss, they sold cigarettes, chased down the boys who were late returning their bicycles, gave out return times and rent rates and took the orders from the cafe—this last job was usually for the shorter boy, which was probably why he insisted on wearing the strange long apron.

The barber was engrossed in trimming the beard of a customer. I guessed the customer was the guard at the water-pump station, because there was a flash-light and a wide-brimmed straw hat on the chair next to him. The barber whispered something about me in the customer's ear, avoiding eye contact with me to dissemble.

'Good evening,' I said to the barber, and contin-ued on my way to the market.

AFFIRMATION OF SILENCE

She said

We all started to sleep in one room, the Hadj, my mother and I.

It was the second winter when the kitchen roof started to leak—right above where my mother slept.

At first she kept it to herself, until a rainy noon when the Hadj discovered the situation. He reprimanded her and insisted that she move into the room with us. She resisted at first, but eventually obeyed his wish.

The Hadj slept at the far end of the room, and my mother and I slept in the opposite corner.

We lived like that until she died. She was ill for three days and nights. Bouts of fever came over her, short waves in quick succession, with the Hadj next to her and me in the doorway. The Hadj never left the room but to do prayers and ablutions, or during the visit of the doctor who examined her and prescribed her medication which the Hadj found in Jericho through the help of one of his friends.

He was weak and afraid, like someone who wakes in the morning to find he knows nothing.

He tried to remember; he squeezed the deep wrinkles on his forehead and coiled his body to pass through a narrow tunnel.

He was unable to do it, though it was necessary for him. It was so necessary it was terrifying.

He gave her water and medicine. He changed her compresses and fed her with his hands. When not doing that, he chanted the Quran endlessly, tracking the desires in her eyes. Everything in the house bowed in submission—the air, the bench, the Christ's thorn at the corner of the courtyard, the doorway and prayer mats, the water pitchers for ablution, the straw mat, the long string of prayer beads in his hand, the three basil seedlings and I.

My mother shut her eyes and went into a new absence.

On the final night, after the Sura of the Ranks, I heard her mutter some words. Only my name reached me. The Hadj was silent a long while, then I heard him. It was him, but in a strange voice, some other voice, not his at all. The voice passed through him and diffused into the space of the room, over me and over my mother.

'Bear witness, Hadja.'

Then I heard her murmur the *shahada* twice.

Then she was silent.

Then the Hadj recited, 'O composed soul, return to your Lord contenting and contented, enter among my servants and enter my Garden . . .'

In his recitation, the Hadj affirmed and extended the silence.

He did not wake me then. He stayed seated near her head and recited, in his new voice, until the sun rose.

The Hadj did not wake me and I did not sleep.

AN EDGE TO EVERY THING
COMES FORWARD

I said

The scent came from the far edge of the river, a thick fragrance of guava furrowing the air and diffusing, then suspending, serene and wet, above us. I left one darkness behind in the alleys and houses, a darkness clogged with the familiar, the traces and smells of people, their sleep and their breath, the lingering movements of their bodies in shadow, the perishing inaudible echo of their words, hanging, falling, vanishing with an unseeing movement of the darkness.

The darkness of people and houses opened into a second darkness now, a neighbouring, different darkness of isolated fields down to the river's edge. A darkness filled with the breathing of plants, with the rustling of fruits as they grew and moved, a savage and wild darkness where the eyes of wandering dogs shone on the irrigated earth, where wilds of primal air collapsed and converged.

'Good evening,' I said to the Bedouin policeman at the turn-off to his watch station. He hesitated and uttered, 'Who's there?'

As I went forward into the light so he could see me, I said, 'It's me.'

He hesitated again and stammered, 'Hot night.'

'Yes,' I said.

Then I went back to the house. The barber was behind me shaking off his towel, then the bicycle renter, followed by the two boys, the tall one carrying a turned-over tin can and the short one with a tray of tea. Then came the policeman and the coachman's daughter, in a buggy pulled by a dragon impaled on a spear. Under the wheels of the carriage was a pavement of washed stone. Three strange women ran barefoot over the pavement. The one in the middle kept shouting, 'Good morning, sir! Good morning, sir! Good morning, sir!'

At the thresholds of houses, on the low walls, on irrigation works and pools, the dead sat quietly, smiling under the weight of their dust and staring as my small demonstration passed by. I went towards her, wherever she was. Dogs barked and heads appeared in the darkness, vanishing once they became whole. Children emerged from the reeds.

Far away, but within my vision, a dense line of darkness advanced, dust on the road, like a great edge, a boundary to every thing.

She said

At dawn of the second day after her burial, I brought him some breakfast on the bench: olives, thyme, oil, bread and tea. Before sitting, he called me and gestured for me to sit across from him. We were alone now for the first time. Husband and wife. She was not with us; we were without her, without her silent creeping movements and her rapt attention to everything. He said, 'From now on, you must not trouble yourself.'

He rose at dawn just as he had every day, alone and weightless and silent. He no longer told stories and I no longer saw. He spent most of his time in the mosque where he performed all five prayers in their entirety, met with his friends and carried out his distant business—agreeing, taking, giving, tolerating.

Silence came from everywhere and set down around us, beat its invisible wings in the air between us and above us. Silence always came from the open doorway and the alley. Silence from the window high on the bedroom wall and silence over the short courtyard fence. Dust too came towards the house, converging in far-off fields, swarming in flight towards the house and the Hadj and me. There was no one there but us now. Those people he used to bring to the house at dawn to sit on the bench or in the evening, in the doorway, had vanished now. They went back to their tombs and their eras. Only he and I remained.

Once he called out to me. It was a week after her death. He was standing in the doorway and I was inside. He motioned for me to sit, was silent a moment, then muttered, 'Good, may God make it good . . . Last night I saw the deceased in a dream.'

This confused me at first. I didn't know if 'the deceased' meant his first wife or my mother.

'My mother?' I said.

'She entrusted you to me, Glory be to God. She appeared to me in your age and your youth and was content.'

I wanted him to speak. I wanted to hear him. Suddenly I felt my love for his voice.

I said, 'Please tell me, Hadj, about Asma, Asma daughter of Abu Bakr, Asma of the Two Sashes.'

The Hadj was silent, then cleared his throat and said, 'Prayers upon the Prophet of the Arabs . . .

'By God, prayer and peace upon Muhammad.'

The Hadj started to speak. As if he started to reappear after having vanished a long time. His voice sounded hesitant, then rushed little by little into the story, very far away into the desert. Around Mecca, the traits of a young girl took shape in guarded and ambiguous space—Asma, carrying the Prophet's bread as she climbed towards the cave where he had fled from his banishers.

The Hadj said, 'Think of the force that protected the Prophet and the Message. Think of the force: first, the spider and her delicate home woven at the entrance of the cave. Then, the two pigeons that built their nest and sheltered there.

'And that little girl, Asma, who had to face the indomitable desert and the non-believers with their sinful hearts.'

I said, 'Glory to God!'

I said

My mother was a fastidious woman. She filled our life with advice and admonitions, mostly pointless. She stacked the house with dried goods and pre-served food for no apparent reason. Things piled up on the floor tripping our feet, or hung down from the ceiling bumping against our heads as we crept through the narrow rooms.

I thought constantly of my mother, with her strange wisdom and constant, obscure fear of what went on around us, her absolute lack of trust in every-day life. I thought of all these things that multiplied around and above us, changing the colour of the ground and walls, the light and the shadow, all these dried and shrivelling things of no clear necessity.

My mother was a Christian from the villages around Nazareth. She had a child from a previous marriage, before her marriage with my father. My father was a Muslim from the mountains and was also married previously and had a child, before marrying my mother. The nickname 'the Christian' stuck to him because of a crucifix of olive wood that he wore around his neck since before the migration, given to him by my mother when he worked in the fields of her village, before their marriage. He kept wearing the cross on his chest and we carried the nickname.

Once, with three friends, he sneaked away, back to her village. They crawled across the borders on their bellies as bullets from both sides whistled above them. They kept crawling day and night, until they were 'there'.

Once 'there', they did not find the village or the houses. Only the road was visible in the town square, the road and the cacti. Cacti were everywhere, covering everything. There were also scattered stones, huge and carved, among the trunks of uprooted trees. The corpses of trees covered the landscape, felled and settled at the bottom of slopes. There was one pomegranate tree left that he could remember. Maybe it remained there because he had remembered it so intensely, even from his new place among us after the migration.

He filled his breast pocket with pomegranates and returned with the three men. The pomegranate juice stained his torso and his clothes as he crawled, and ran down onto the narrow, twisting road.

From far off, when they reached the flatlands, the cacti looked like giant green fruits, plucked and strung above the lean road. Later, he kept on asking himself, and asking us too, 'Why did only the road remain?'

He wanted to turn that question into a marvel, a philosophy, an intended message he could believe in.

When he arrived at night, he was spotted with pomegranate juice. He was at the same time afraid and joyful. He stood, damp, with the one uncrushed fruit in his hand. He was almost crying when he said, 'It is from *there*.'

He placed it on our only table, and the fruit stayed there. We were unable to wound it. We were afraid to cause it, or him, pain. It was in front of us— breathing and remembering—on that squat table, next to the knife that my youngest sister had brought and about which we quickly forgot. It was impossible for us to go beyond that. The fruit was completely alive and necessary for him, his only means to make us believe him, to make us believe all those stories that he had brought to us—of his house, his village and his land.

Our house, our village, our land.

He carried no picture, no key or sign of those things except one cross of olive wood that he wore on his chest. The pomegranate was necessary for him to continue remembering, a very small way station, but one he needed to keep on walking. Perhaps for this reason my mother never approached the fruit either, because she feared that if he woke up one day and didn't find it on the table, he would go back there again.

As for the fruit itself, it seemed that she had been destined to come precisely to this place, that she also knew she had been wronged and afraid and far away, like us.

At night, when everyone was asleep, after my mother and father went to bed, I heard the pome-granate breathing on the table. As soon as I shut my eyes, I felt a movement, far away and visible, among the cactus clusters—peoples' heads, minarets, house windows, balconies with potted flowers—emerging between dense cactus sheets and descending, with caution, the sinuous described road, towards us.

From that night on, his tone started to change. His speech filled with details, details of everything, of houses and plants, the names and ages of boys and girls, cooking smells from houses and names of flowers on balconies, weddings, and the pictures hung on walls. At night, in summer or winter, he would sit and bring those things out from beneath dense cactus groves, would brush them free of dust and thorns and time with intense care.

From then on, the story changed too. He no longer began it with careful hesitation. He became freer and the things themselves were more full of the desire to remain, had the power to preserve their own recollections, to contribute to the renewal of their description, depiction and affirmation. This happened as the pomegranate watched with deep satisfaction from her place on the table, near the forgotten knife my little sister had brought.

Sometimes I watched them as they stole glances at each other and exchanged satisfaction—he and the fruit.

He became more convinced of the things that happened to him and to us. He was more in possession of the force of description, more able to bring out the furnishings forgotten beneath the forest of cacti, to amass them in the two rooms where we breathed.

The house began to fill anew with his memories. The new objects amassed on the floor, hung from the walls and doors and ceiling, dangled above us as we stumbled and crashed our faces into everything. The pomegranate watched from the table, giving its fruitful assistance as he brought back all he could carry from that deep well that brought him and it together.

Just above the pomegranate was Saint George. My mother had brought him back from her church. Saint George reached out to the fruit and to us with stories and memories and voices. We sat inside the house and stared at all this from the tops of piles, beneath great necklaces and hanging chains of shrivelling goods.

Far away, the cacti shed their sheets and rose like a lake of green thorns on the hill, as the road flashed and fell, narrow and twisting and cautious.

At night, when the pomegranate began to breathe and Saint George dismounted his horse, leaving the dragon to bleed to death, and when Husseini loosed the two bullet belts from his chest— it was then that hundreds of heads and eyes and windows and balconies and minarets came down from among the cactus forest and descended the road, towards our house.

HIS ABSENCE

She **said**

We were on our own. He was alone, maintaining his distance every day. I was alone. I flicked my hand against a silence that called to some part of him and came towards our lone house.

I knew that it was him sprinkling water at dawn on the three seedlings of basil before he went off to the mosque.

Then he started to disappear and grow more distant. I could not fight it, this continuously growing distance, the silence piling everywhere, on the doorway, the bench, the window, the clothing, on the bed sheets, in the words, in the air. So I stopped resisting completely.

On that morning, I gathered my dress that was torn to the waist, as I told you, and went to the third doorway on the right. I went to your doorway to tell you that he was dead. I wanted you to be sad for that reason.

That was necessary for me.

Very necessary.

NO LONGER NECESSARY

I said

She was still lying on her back, with her eyes closed. A light redness crossed her face and granted it a sign of indistinguishable age. Her face looked strange and far away, impossible to realize, a going that promised nothing, that led to no arrival.

The tension marking her jaws faded, and her skin flowed, dark and brown. I saw a bronze flash, like a loose cord, at the top of her cheek. So she could hear me, I said, 'You will stay beautiful for a hundred years.'

She turned her uncoiling body to the wall and her incredible black hair fell over half her face. For an instant, a lock of pure white hair flashed like a horse from nowhere, then was gone.

She was far away and silent, against the wall. I was in the corner, alone and afraid. She looked but didn't see me. I didn't look but I saw her. We were alone in the Hadj's house—her house, his house.

She said, 'Why are you dressed? You can sleep until morning prayers. I'll wake you.'

A carnal urge wrapped her voice now, held me and the room, the noon tea and the night of the ring. I was afraid that she was naked and that we were alone. I was able to accept everything without desire, empty and suspended in the urge, stripped away from everything that enveloped me, except her.

I said, 'You sleep, take your rest. I don't want to sleep.'

She moved without rising, moved to the bed, and straightened it. Then she stretched out on the bed, leaving most of the space for me.

Like someone remembering, she said, 'The tea, I placed it by the window. Take it on your way out.'

From where I was, I said, 'There's no need for that. It is no longer necessary. Why don't you sleep?'

Then she remembered again, 'Don't forget the tea, for the morning.'

I said, 'It was not for me. It was for my mother. She is dead now.'

She said without hearing me, 'Don't forget it, you will need it.'

I said without seeing her, 'I don't think so. I told you. It is no longer necessary . . . '

She slept. Her chest rose and fell regularly. She was in the farthest room of sleep. A strand of saliva flowed from the corner of her mouth and wet the pillow. A light reflected on the ceiling from where she was now, there, in her sleep. It was reflected on the reeds in the ceiling, the reeds bound tightly together so many years ago with cords left over from the military encampment. It was on a day when we were all here, he and I and the Hadj and the others.

We were building the house. It was a few weeks after she married the Hadj, after he decided to move from his house near the river to here. She was greater than us. She prepared tea and carried it to the elders under the oak tree and to the workers on the roof. She never passed by us in the wondrous domes of newspaper we had made ourselves to shelter from the sun. The two of us were on the ground, each drawing his knife over the length of each reed until the edge hit the node from which the new shoot protruded. Husks flew about as the knives surged to new nodes, turned briskly in our fingers and slid over the smooth body's surface.

We competed for no prize. He was always ahead of me. His pile of reeds grew quickly by his side. The Hadj approached us to praise my work and his effort. He pointed to my small, extremely neat pile and said, with a laughter that came from the depths of his heart, 'These are for the bedroom.'

Then he pointed to his larger pile, less gleaming, and said, 'And these are for the kitchen.'

He laughed again, and so did the elders beneath the oak tree and the workers on the roof. She smiled, wherever she was, and he and I were satisfied. The Hadj mixed the piles together and handed them to the men on the roof, where they fixed the trunks straight as bridges and laid down the reeds which they bound, piece by piece, into a thick, multiplying thatch held together with those tough military cords.

I stared as the pile grew higher. I saw my reeds glimmer on the earth beneath the shelter, hopeful and content. He sang a bawdy song at the top of his voice. The sheikhs under the oak tree goaded him on and the workers on the roof answered his song.

She was shy, wherever she was. The Hadj laughed and moved about everywhere; he was on the ground and then on the ladder, then his head appeared by the roof's edge, chiding or encouraging, praising or scolding, then he was back under the oak tree, sipping his tea audibly among the sheikhs.

Everything was on its way towards completion. I was going towards death. The Hadj was dead. And he had drowned in the river some time ago. She slept as I stared at the roof of reeds we had husked on that burning hot day. I remembered and looked to the light that came from her sleep and was refracted on the reeds up the ceiling. I loosed them, reed by reed, and brought them back down the ladder into our hands that held short knives. It was there that I would know—

Him. Me. Him. Him.
Him. Me. Him. Him.
Him. Him. Me. Me.
Him.

The five chairs on which the elders sat beneath the oak had disappeared, undone in a fog that rose from the earth underneath them. Their seated figures evaporated, leaving only voices and the sounds of sipping tea at five invisible points in fog. Above, the fog multiplied until the thatch on the roof and the steps of the ladder came apart. There were only three bodies emitting light. Three bodies remained from that time. Pouring light.

He and I are wrapped in the absence of the others, bent over two long reeds, rowing into white water.

Close by us, there, at the far end of time, her body sits and emanates light, waiting for the completion of our death.

Me. Him. Him. Him. Me. Me. Him.
Him.

★

Tunisia, 1991